Camp Crush
A Self-Insert Novella

Krista Coleman

Reading Instructions

This is a self-insert story.
That means every time you see
a line (_____) you insert your name.
Have fun being the protagonist!

Contents

Chapter One: Reset

You just finished your first year of teaching; that was an accomplishment considering the district you were in! But you knew, after such an experience, maybe teaching wasn't for you. It wasn't the kids. You knew everyone had their individual needs and quirks, which made them each dear to you. But the administration had strict reviews from biased supervisors and ideals about "teaching to the test" that weren't your cup of tea. *You couldn't help the kids learn if you couldn't be creative!*

So, just when you thought you'd be enjoying your first free summer as an educator, you found yourself scouring for possible jobs. And it was already July. Where could one with your expertise go? When you were sipping your morning coffee, you saw an oak tree symbol in a newspaper ad. *A camp counselor…* Well, you were one of those when you were back in high school. That was part of the reason you became a teacher in the first place. You believed in hands-on learning: experiencing the science and art of nature firsthand.

As a kid you'd thought you'd become a park ranger. A camp counselor was a similar career path, right? You'd be outside. You'd still be able to help kids learn about nature. Best of all, there would be none of that standardized testing you had come to despise. *Why not give this job a try for the summer?* Convinced, you dialed the number from the ad.

"Hello?" the line picked up with a tired man's low voice.

"Hello, is this Camp Oak?"

"Yes it- Jessie! Put that down!" the voice responded. There were several moments of scuffled silence where you wondered what was going on.

"I'm sorry about that," a cheery male voice answered. "Atticus had to step out for a second. This is Doran. How may I help you?"

"Um, is this Camp Oak?"

"Why, yes it is! What interests you in our fine establishment?"

"I saw in an ad that you might need assistance; and, well, heard it," you laughed.

His laugh was a sweet one. "Yes, I think an extra set of hands would be good around here. The kids can get a little antsy halfway through the summer at sleepaway camp."

"Oh, I know how kids can get when the weather is warm. I'm… I was a teacher this past year."

"Wow! A teacher?!" The man's voice became excited. "And you want to help us?"

"I would like to."

"We would love to have you!"

"Really?"

"Really. Give us some time to check your qualifications and it should be a cinch!"

"Thanks. I look forward to meeting you, Doran."

"Likewise."

You felt excited about starting a new chapter of your life as you drove towards the camp with butterflies in your stomach. You wondered what the living arrangements would be like. But most of all, you wondered about the people. What would these kids be like?

How would your co-counselors act? Were they younger than you? You hoped that they were capable of leading the group of children. Did they have a disciplinary structure? You didn't want to carry the whole camp on your back. But, from the sounds of what occurred on the phone, you wondered if you just might.

It was early in the morning when you pulled up in the gravel parking lot near the flagpole. "_____!" A man greeted you with a smile from outside your window. He was in his late twenties with soft ocean eyes and even softer looking wavy auburn hair. You marveled at how he had such enthusiasm so early. You'd even struggled with that as a teacher.

"Hello," you stepped out. "You must be Doran?"

"That's me!" The corners of his mouth turned up. "And this is Atticus!" He turned to point beside him, but no one was there. You followed Doran's finger back to the main cabin door. A tan man in his mid-twenties with tousled short black hair gave you a head nod. "Yo."

"Hey," you smiled back. Your co-workers were easy on the eyes.

Doran clasped his hands. "The kids will be up in a second for breakfast. Oh! They will be so excited to meet you, _____. First, let me show you your cabin."

"My own cabin?" Your eyes grew wide with anticipation.

"Yes. We separate staff cabins by gender identity. Unfortunately, we have more males than females this year. We are glad to have you, by the way."

"Great. Thank you, Doran." You saw him smile at your use of his name. That one had a praise kink for sure. "Show me the way and I'll drop off my bags."

"Boys and girls," Doran announced over the mess hall at breakfast, "everyone, I would like to have our new friend here introduce herself." He stepped back to give you the floor.

"Hello kids, you can call me Ms._____ and I will be here to assist-"

"Wait, wait, wait," a girl with curly blonde hair and dark eyes stood up. "Miss? What are you, a teacher?"

"Well, I did teach the past year at-"

The crowd of middle school aged children collectively groaned. "This isn't fair!"

"Now, Jessie," Doran gave a semi-disciplinary tone; the same that Mister Rogers would be capable of.

"No, Doran! Not only do I have no choice in attending this camp, but I also don't even have a summer! This bullshit is school part two!"

You blinked at the age-inappropriate language and looked to the other staff for guidance. Atticus's shrug stated that this was accepted behavior.

"Textbooks?!" A dark-skinned girl's hazel eyes shrunk in terror as she stood on the table. "I didn't sign up for this! I thought summer camps were about games and friendship!"

A stocky kid with glasses politely raised his arm, "Are they science textbooks?"

"Oh, for Pete's sake- there are no textbooks!" you corrected. "But I was a biology teacher this past year."

Doran looked at you interestedly.

"Ah man, I was looking for something like computer science." The kid with glasses sat back down disappointedly. "I'm more interested in technology than biology."

"What do you mean?" You put your hands on your hips. "Life science has tons of technology! Why, if you go to the nearest hospital you'll find-"

"Augh!" Jessie tilted her head back. "She's as bad as Doran!"

"Really?" you questioned. "What does he do?"

"He tries to teach us lessons about pinecones and crap."

You looked over at your coworker. It appeared someone else had once wanted to be a park ranger.

After a long day spent playing cops and robbers, you began to get an idea of the campers' personalities. It played out like something from the Stanford Prison Experiment. There was clearly a lack of rules at camp: it was survival of the bullies. When the day was over and the flag was lowered, the kids returned to their cabins. At least those conditions weren't bad. They had wooden bunks and common rooms decorated with TVs and furniture. After bidding the kids goodnight, you turned to your coworkers.

"All right, counselor meeting."

Doran's sea-colored eyes lit up. "Good idea, _____ ! Usually, we just go our separate ways to grab dinner before we get some shut eye. It would be great to talk about the events of the day."

Atticus was already walking off when you put a hand on his arm. "Wha-?" He pulled out an earbud. "Ah man, I was just about to catch up on a new horror podcast."

"After we talk, you can share your podcast with me if you want. Sounds good?"

"Okay," he looked you over. "But I'm not sure it's your taste. Hope you can handle it."

You all sat in the male counselor's cabin. Atticus lounged on the bed while Doran took the office chair near the desk. You opted for leaning against the desk. You counted three beds. "Is there another counselor?"

"Nah, just the handyman," Atticus answered.

"I hope I get to meet Mr. Mysterious," you said. "So, let me get this straight- are there rules here?"

Atticus and Doran cringed at one another. Doran spoke first, "Well, _____, we just want to be friendly with the campers and give them the summer that they deserve."

"Friendly, but not their friend, right?"

"Wouldn't it be good if we could all be friends?" Doran looked up to you with a vulnerable expression.

You recalled being that innocent as a student teacher. "Doran," you laughed, "do you have any kid friends that you hang out with at home?"

Doran looked down for a moment, his smile fading, "No, of course not."

It seemed like he didn't have much of a home to speak of. "These kids need structure: discipline. For example, are there any punishments for stealing another camper's lunch?"

Atticus let out a snort. "I know who you're talking about. And yes, we've tried to set up discipline for Billy. It was hilarious."

You inclined your head, "What do you mean?"

"Doran here was acting like a drill sergeant!" Atticus snickered. "But all the kids could see through him and knew he wasn't a threat."

"You?" you turned to look at the slim man with awe. As you imagined him in form-fitting military uniform you couldn't help but envision a more commanding side to Doran. The thought made you swallow in thirst rather than hold your stomach in laughter. You always did have a thing for men in uniforms (even if it was just roleplay).

A rosy color dusted his pale complexion. "It wasn't that bad."

"Yes it was," Atticus regained his breath after laughing. "You couldn't get him to do anything. We've still got to watch Jessie like a hawk, so she doesn't steal your phone again." He looked at you, "For the campers, Camp Oak is cell phone free. We keep them in a box in the front office."

"I see."

"But, seriously, _____, we are lacking in that department. Anything we try just blows up in our faces. It's not like we can beat it out of them."

You laughed, "Atticus! Did I hear right that you have a degree in psychology? We don't have to!"

He smiled, "Well, it wasn't early child psychology, Teach. It was criminal."

"Kids are kind of like tiny adults. Hell, Jessie is already postulating at an advanced level... I need some more time to figure her out."

"We all do," Doran rested his chin in his palm.

You felt for his despondent look. "Let me share with you something I learned from school. What do you think is the best way to approach discipline as a parent?"

"It's not whooping ass?" Atticus joked.

"Being optimistic?" Doran tilted his head.

"Gather 'round," you approached a rolling chalkboard. "There are four different parenting types." You watched as Doran's eyes lit up and Atticus seemed interested since it was sort of his field as well. "Authoritarian, Authoritative, Permissive, and Uninvolved. Now, let's take a look at your previous answers. *Whooping ass* and being a drill sergeant," you looked Atticus over, "would fall under Authoritarian. These parents are strict and controlling; they require obedience. Their authority is absolute and cannot be questioned for any reason."

Atticus nodded. "I guess that's true."

"And do you know what happens to these kids?" you asked.

Doran shook his head.

"They become timid, have low self-esteem, and rely on someone else's judgment." You put a line through the word. "Now we're going to address your style, Doran: Permissive."

"Oh!" Atticus hooted in judgment at Doran, who stared in defiance.

"Maybe it's good," he harrumphed.

"Permissive parents are warm and accepting," you continued as he beamed. Too bad that his beautiful smile wouldn't last long. "They ask little of their children and avoid confrontation. They are not at all demanding, the complete opposite of Authoritarian. Unfortunately, they are often out of touch with the child, or they are parenting this way because of what they lacked as children. They bend over backwards for the kids and give them whatever they want."

Atticus gave Doran a sly smile.

"If the parent is too lax, the child has no boundaries. It can become chaotic, since the kid *does* need some form of guidance. The child can feel alone or ignored because the parent can be perceived as indifferent."

Doran stood up and you stepped back under his height. He was a head taller than you. "I'd never want that." You gave him the stub of chalk to cross out the word for himself. His hand was warm as it brushed yours. He had passion; that much was clear to see.

"Uninvolved," you continued on from your spot back at the table as Doran stood at the chalkboard. "Well, the name speaks for itself. You demand nothing and provide nothing. The child has absolute freedom. This is the worst style because it can become neglect."

Doran crossed out the word and you smiled. You'd never had a teacher's pet before. "So, what's the right choice?"

"Authoritative." Atticus observed the only word left.

"This one takes all the good parts and puts them together: warmth and communication." You touched Doran's bicep in acknowledgement. "Demanding and responsive," you stood by Atticus. "They're assertive but not intrusive or restrictive." You smiled at Doran. "You expect social responsibility and self-regulation as well as cooperation. While your expectations are high, you encourage discourse and freedom of expression. Set clear boundaries that cannot be crossed but allow them to question why these boundaries are in place. Establish what the punishments and rewards are; let them decide. Though this should take place far in advance of their actions."

"You've got some impressive knowledge," Doran remarked. "You would make a good parent, _____."

"Thanks, but I'm not trying to be," you laughed as you brushed the hair out of your face.

"But how do we set punishments and rewards halfway through the summer?" Atticus asked.

"Well," you took your seat on the table, "sometimes even the best parents or camp counselors need a reset day."

"Tomorrow," Doran nodded, taking a seat beside you. You noticed how his warm leg brushed against yours hanging over the side. "And we'll go forward from there." The look on his face was enough to give you sweet dreams.

Chapter Two: Retry

Jessie sat behind her tray at breakfast, eyeing you, as she spoke to her friends. "Josh, do you think she's up to something?"

The glasses wearing boy sipped on his juice box. "What do you mean?"

"She didn't do anything yesterday. She just sat and observed, like some sort of robot."

"I don't know. But at least she knows science. Even if it's the," he cringed, "dissection kind. I'll take what I can get."

Jessie shook her ponytail. "Fuckin' traitor. Aisha, what do you think of Miss Prim-and-Proper?"

The girl with box braids spoke between shovels of food, "Oh, I thought her name was Ms. _____."

Jessie gave her a blank stare. "Aisha, it's a figure of... never mind. You hate school. Want to revolt?"

"Nah. It's not that I hate school, I'm just better at sports and hands-on things."

Jessie pinched the bridge of her nose. "Okay. Looks like I'm going solo on this one. I'll be damned if I relive that stupid school year." As soon as she turned to see the three counselors standing at the front of the room, the pit of her stomach told her it was too late.

"Good morning campers," you greeted the room. "We're going to start with a little activity. You will each have two cards with your names." Doran and Atticus started passing around green and red index cards. "On the green card, I want you to write three things you would love to do or play or eat. Save the best one for last. On the red card, I'd like you to put three things you would hate to do or play or eat. Maybe some chores or vegetables, for example. Be reasonable and honest."

"Why?" Jessie spoke up, "So you can blackmail us?"

"So, we can get to know you better!" Doran smiled.

"This activity is optional, Jessie," you responded. "But, if you don't fill in anything, just remember we'll be guessing for you."

"Fine by me." Jessie spoke as she kicked back and watched her campmates write.

"Okay, looks like everyone is done. Please hand them forward."

The campers shuffled the cards down the benches toward the front of the room.

"Now," you held them aloft, "these will serve as your punishments and rewards."

"What a twist!" one small girl camper named Amy pulled back dramatically.

"Hostile takeover," Billy commented as his dark eyes shone, "I admire you."

"This isn't a takeover," you waved your hand, "this is just structure: to help you feel safe. Nobody wants to be bullied or to be put in danger. Right?"

The crowd gave a mixed response of indifference.

You cringed. "Look at it this way," you held up the card, "if you do something good, you'll get a reward that was chosen by you!"

Jessie leaned forward, "So you'll be guessing for me, then."

"Yup," you smiled.

"What if I don't like it?"

"That's the downside of not participating. But the counselors should know you. So, if we give you something you don't like, you can make us do a chore we don't like. We've also filled out the two cards. Sounds fair?"

"Oh yeah." A smirk came to her face.

"But how will we know what's good and bad?" Aisha raised her hand.

"I'm glad you asked. Let's set up some rules together. What would make you feel safe and have a good summer?"

"Rules?!" Jessie stood up, "*Fuck* the rules."

The other campers looked to you for your response. "One," you wrote on the same rolling chalkboard, "The colorful language can stay because it helps you express yourself. As long as you aren't hurting anyone else, use your vocabulary to your advantage. Is that the rule you were trying to create, Jessie?"

Her jaw dropped and retracted before she took a seat. She needed more time to think things over.

After a reasonable chart of rules was democratically set up, you took a step back and admired your handiwork. Each kid had colored a rule they found important, while Jessie declined participation.

You pasted it to the wall in the mess hall.

"Now we have a code to abide by!" Doran smiled.

"Maybe we'll finally get some order in this place," Atticus shouldered you playfully.

You sure hoped so, but you knew it would take the kids some time to get used to the idea. "So, what activities do we have on schedule today?" You looked at Doran.

"It's Ropes Course Day!" He said enthusiastically to a tepid response from the crowd. Aisha actually appeared excited. "Oh! I'm a good climber, Ms. _____! Watch me climb!"

"Of course," you smiled warmly. "But you don't need to call me Miss. _____ is fine."

"Don't trust her, Aisha," Jessie spoke up. "It only took her so long to take out the index cards and chalkboard. Soon comes the Number 2 pencils and mind-numbing worksheets."

"Ugh," you stuck out your tongue, "worksheets."

"What the hell do you mean *ugh*? Aren't worksheets, like, on your green index card?"

"Wouldn't you like to know what's on my card," you teased. "But no. They'd probably be on the red one."

Jessie gave you a squinty look. "You must have been a failure as a teacher."

"Depends on who you ask," you smiled with a shrug.

You all gathered outside the ropes course where you saw a buff man in his early thirties was checking the equipment. He had short blonde hair and a neatly trimmed beard. His tank revealed his toned arms and chest as well as some pine shaped tattoos. He looked like someone who did a lot of hiking. *The man was a member of the camp, right?* Someone had brewed an early pot of coffee that morning; it must have been him.

You tilted your head in acknowledgement. "Mr. Mysterious?"

"Name's Zephan. But you can call me Z."

"That suits you," you looked him up and down as you shook his hand.

"Sorry I've been incognito; I was just gathering supplies from town. I'm kind of a jack of all trades around here. I do the cooking and the cleaning."

"Are you the gym teacher, as well?"

He laughed. "God, no. I leave that to Atticus and Doran."

"Is this safe for the kids?" you glanced at the course.

"Safe enough for me to jump up and down on. Believe me, I don't want any lawsuits."

"Right." You looked up into the trees. It was about ten feet high and fifteen feet across. There were helmets for everyone and an old, thick gym mat underneath. So, if it all went to hell, injuries wouldn't be that bad. You smiled at your memories of once completing a similar course. Teamwork: that's what the exercise was all about. After working together this morning, it was a great opportunity to continue on the right track.

The kids put on their safety equipment and took a seat while Doran explained how to work a carabiner. Something about the way his hands expertly moved across the length of the rope had you lost in thought: *what else were those hands capable of?*

It was kind of naughty of you to think that way, but as long as it stayed inside your head it wasn't hurting anyone. You imagined the ropes crisscrossing over your body, tightening around your midsection just beneath your breasts and stealing a breath from you as the auburn-haired man spoke in soothing tones about how to tie the knots, as if you weren't naked before him.

"_____?"

You blinked as Doran and Aisha stared at you inquisitively. "Yes?" you tried to sound normal.

"Could you get the other kids ready while I spot Aisha?"

"Of course!" You responded as you lined the children up at the base of the course.

"You're a space cadet, aren't you?" Jessie mocked.

"I can be," you grinned. "Come to think of it, have you ever thought about what it's like in the vacuum of space?"

"Ah! Ah! Ah!" Jessie plugged her ears and glared at you. "I don't want to hear a science lesson. Talk to Josh."

Soon, all of the children were lined up on the ropes. Billy was shaking the rope. Jessie yelled at him before she helped Amy to stand on the platform. After some trials and tribulations, the kids were ready to help each other down.

14

Jessie volunteered to be the last one remaining in order to assist everybody. She looked to you to see if you acknowledged her efforts. You gave her a nod and smile to show that you did. It was good to see her behaving well, even if she had external motivations. You wondered what reward to provide. Perhaps you could ask Atticus or Doran to pick it for her, since they had known her longer.

"I'm so proud of you, Jessie!" Doran called as Atticus helped on belay. Doran was such a softy. It was touching to see him so happy. Maybe he knew the most about Jessie after all.

"Good job, Jessie! You get a reward." You held up your hand for a high five, which she ignored.

"Yeah, yeah. So, what do I get?" she peeked up at you from under her bangs.

"Well, I think Doran could provide you with something you'd really-"

"Not happening."

You noticed Doran's drop in expression.

"You should know me," Jessie continued, "as you said. So, let me hear it."

"Well," your lips turned into a thin line as you examined your co-counselor's fearful faces. "I can honestly say that I don't know you Jessie, not really. But I would like to." You examined her face, which told you she already suspected as much. "I will take a guess and say... you would like to have a campfire tonight?"

She laughed as she wiped her eyes. "You really have no idea. I'm staying as far away from Doran's guitar solos as I possibly can."

"Well, at least I learned something about you," you smiled.

She took a moment to examine you. "Red card please." She waved her fingers, as if asking you to insert cash.

"Looks like I'm the first to be punished," you handed it over.

"And by your own system no less," Amy said in a tiny voice.

"We'll go in order from least to worst," you encouraged.

"Oh no, you didn't specify that beforehand. I'm going straight to last on the list: you're cleaning the latrines."

You sighed. "All right Jessie, you're right."

She blinked at your admission.

"I didn't specify. But we will do so going forward. Deal?"

"Deal."

As you were arm deep in yellow gloves and cleaning away you heard the sound of a camera snap behind you.

"Hey!" You turned around to see Jessie with a smartphone. You lidded your eyes and returned to your duties. "I thought kids weren't allowed to have phones out here."

"We're not, really. This is Doran's phone. I borrowed it."

"Doran's?" you flushed. "What did you borrow it for?"

"He just leaves it out on the windowsill of the mess hall. It's begging to be stolen. I use it for whatever I want."

"What's that?"

"You want me to tell you my nefarious plans? No way."

"No," you stopped scrubbing. "I'd like you to tell me what you want. I'd really like to know."

"You're a lot like Dork-an." *That must have been her nickname for Doran.*

"I'm glad," you hummed as you returned to work.

"Glad? Why the hell are you glad? He's annoying as fuck."

"At least he cares, right?"

"You think he cares? He's just like all the other adults putting on some sham authority act to make you believe in him. He just happens to play a goody-goody really well."

16

You thought about her words. "So, you're saying he's too good to be true?"

"Exactly. Without the positive connotations."

"Maybe you're right. You read people pretty well."

"...Really?" she questioned.

"A lot of adults are putting on an act of confidence or happiness because they don't know what they're doing with their lives. But do you really want to be right in this case?"

"I don't- I don't know."

"He might be putting on a happy face, but I could see no reason he would fake caring about any of you kids."

"I've been trying to figure that one out myself." She looked away from you.

"I'll tell you what, I'll work with you to find out if he really cares. If he doesn't, then we'll both make him suffer." You knew the errand was futile, but it would be good for Jessie to see that adults could truly care.

"Yeah," she smiled back at you genuinely. "I'd like that. In the meantime, I'm going to show the camp what you look like knee-deep in toilets."

"Thanks Jessie."

"My pleasure!"

Chapter Three: Realize

"Hey, Doran."

"Jessie! What are you doing in the mess hall this late? Isn't it lights out?"

"I borrowed your phone. Thought you might like to look at the pictures I took today."

"You borrowed my..." Doran patted his pockets, "Oh I see. Why, isn't that thoughtful of you- sharing your photos with me." He reached for the phone.

"Wait," Jessie held it back. "Before I give it to you, I'm curious; what would you have given me as a reward earlier?"

"Well, I'd have given you the afternoon off from camp activities."

"Damn," Jessie clicked her tongue at the missed opportunity. "Why? Don't you like comradery and all that?"

"I do. But wasn't this supposed to be about what *you* wanted?"

"Whatever. Here's your phone," Jessie threw it over his shoulder as Doran struggled to catch it.

"Oh, I'm excited to see just what you took pictures of. The lake is awfully pretty at night." He swiped through to see a photo of you in a rather provocative position as you scrubbed the toilets on your knees.

Jessie heard Doran gasp as her smirk grew. "She's awfully pretty too, huh Doran?"

Doran looked up with nothing to say as his face conveyed it all.

"Good night, Doran." Jessie turned with a grin. She'd found a new weakness that could work to her advantage.

You saw her walking out of the mess hall. "Jessie!" you called. "What are you doing-"

"Yeah, it's late: blah, blah, blah. I heard it already from Captain Clueless."

"You want me to walk you back? It looks like you don't have a flashlight."

"Eh, why not. I was using the one on the phone earlier."

"You mean you don't have it anymore?"

"Jessie, you get back here!" Doran cried as he exited the hall.

"Doran?" you questioned.

"Oh, Ms. _____! What a surprise to see you standing here!" He laughed oddly, "Not that you'd be kneeling or anything like that, I mean-"

"Kneeling?" Your nose wrinkled.

Jessie stifled a laugh.

"Oh," you looked at the kid knowingly as you crossed your arms. "So that was the picture you wanted to show everyone."

"You showed it to everyone?!" Doran's voice hiked.

"You're the only one that cared, Doran." Jessie smiled. "What does that say about you?"

"That I care about my co-counselor's consent and privacy. I'm afraid you're going to have to be punished for this."

Jessie blinked in realization before she hung her head and kicked the ground. "At least can _____ pick it out? It might be something I enjoy."

"No. I've got the perfect punishment for you."

"What? What could be worse than daily life in this hell hole?"

"You're going to sing a song at a campfire tomorrow night."

"Oh *hell* no. There is no way I'm going to do that. No way-"

"I'm apparently doing this." Jessie spoke at the campfire that night. It was only you, Atticus, and Doran as the rest of the campers were shooed off to sleep. Aisha and Josh lingered behind, but Jessie told them to go on ahead. They knew not to ask questions.

"I didn't want to embarrass you in front of your friends, Jessie." Doran tuned his well-worn guitar. "I know you have an image to uphold. So, I thought this would be best. I know you'll do great."

"Typical Doran. He sets out to punish someone and ends up complimenting them. You really are an idiot. All right, let's get this over with."

"And it's a camp song?" Doran insisted.

"Yes, Dork-an." Jessie bit out. "I think it applies to my situation quite nicely."

Doran strummed as you and Atticus looked on in anxious trepidation. Jessie closed her eyes and sang out:

> *The biscuits that they give us, they say are mighty fine.*
> *But one rolled off the table and killed a friend of mine.*
> *Oh, I don't want to be at summer camp. No! Gee mom, I wanna go,*
> *But they won't let me go, Gee mom I wanna go home!*

You and Atticus exchanged a look of awe as Doran nearly stopped strumming.

"There. Happy?" Jessie crossed her arms as she flopped back onto the log.

"That was great!" Doran exclaimed.

"Shut up." Jessie hunched.

"Nice job, Jessie." Atticus gave two thumbs up.

"Your voice is really something," you marveled.

"Yeah, something awful," she snarked.

"No, really. I think I'll add it to my green index card." You shuffled through your pockets.

"So, help me, _____, I will haunt you until the end of your days if you do. Not a word of this to anyone. Got it?"

Everyone nodded in a silent pact. "Good. I'm going back now."

"We'll walk you," Doran spoke.

"No! Atticus will walk me. I've had enough of the two of you. Later, losers."

"Good night, Jessie!" Doran waved.

You laughed as you stood and held out your hand, "Let's go to bed, Doran."

As soon as he grasped your hand, you felt him pull you down into his chest. You were awkwardly straddling his leg as he held you tightly. You could hear the even beating of his heart as you felt his warmth and the words reverberating from his chest. "That's something I never thought I would see, thank you." He smelled faintly of days in the summer sun.

"It's no big deal, really-"

"It is." He took a breath. "I'm not sure if you know: Jessie is my half-sister."

"Oh!" It was all coming together. "Thank you for letting me know. You don't need to tell me anything more."

"But I find myself wanting to." He looked up at you.

You paused. "Then, I'm here to listen."

He glanced into the fire. "We have the same deadbeat dad. And Jessie's mom seems even less involved than mine was. We've been estranged, so I've been trying to get to know her better: to let her know she has a big brother who cares. But, she has this wall up. One that I can understand." His eyes volleyed back to you. "But I feel like the door is at least partially open now."

"Glad I could help," you pulled back, so your face was even with his. "Doran?"

"Silly me!" he laughed embarrassedly, "There I go forgetting about personal space." He stood slowly to keep you both from falling. "Let's go to bed." He coughed nervously. "In the platonic sense I mean!"

"Of course, Doran." You each contributed to putting out the fire. "Lead the way." You followed his battery-powered lantern as the two of you walked to the sound of crickets and a chorus of frogs. Doran said he'd walked these trails as a boy, back when he was at camp. You imagined him at Jessie's age and the image made you smile. You hoped that she would come to trust her older brother. Someday, it would be nice if she turned out just as well as he did despite the circumstances. Before you knew it, you were at your door. "I had a really good time tonight." You spoke slowly, "You know, I think I'll add your singing voice to my green index card as well."

Doran looked down shyly, "That's nice of you to say."

"I mean it. And you can play the guitar! That's pretty amazing."

"You're pretty amazing yourself." He looked up at you with a soft smile. It rendered you speechless. "I'll see you bright and early. Sweet dreams, _____."

"Sweet dreams, Doran," you replied as you watched him turn to leave.

He looked back over his shoulder once and gave you a wave. You waved back before closing and locking the door. You'd be doing more than dreaming that night.

As Doran lay in his bed that night, leaving one leg out of the blankets in the thick summer air, he couldn't stop thinking about your face. Your eyes looked so soft when you waved to him. You were so warm and kind. He loved how your hair looked, lightly tousled by the summer breeze. You had a smile that could make anybody's knees weak. Normally he would be intimidated, but it felt like he had known you for a long time. He couldn't pinpoint it, but there was something about you that made you click on a different level.

He'd never felt that with another girl. Not that he'd had much experience with girlfriends. Everyone he'd gone out to dinner with had said he came on too strong, or said he smiled too much. The list went on: too innocent, too nice, or too skinny. But, you hadn't rolled your eyes at his enthusiasm. You hadn't made fun of him or given up when the going got tough. You were exactly what this camp needed. He wondered for a moment how Camp Oak had gotten so lucky. *How had he gotten so lucky?*

He was the one that got to work beside you. But all that working beside you had made him sort of selfish, hadn't it? Maybe he'd come to rely on you too much. Maybe all that time together was causing him to take advantage of your closeness. Because no matter how much of your time or praise he had, it made him want more. Your presence was so overwhelmingly attractive that he'd wanted to kiss you. Doran cringed and brought the blankets up to hide his blush. In doing so, he'd revealed another growing problem.

He wanted to touch himself, but you were his coworker. If he pleasured himself to images of you, would that go too far? He'd never had this problem before. He was always so focused on camp. Doran shut his eyes tightly and willed sleep upon himself. If he ignored these feelings, then everything might just go away. After all, there was no way you could feel the same. And he didn't feel like unrequited love this summer. Something told him this time would hurt worse, since he'd see you every day. The fact that he'd see you in the morning calmed him, He could just be happy to be near you. Everything would be okay.

"Good morning, _____!" You heard a cheerful man burst through your doorway.

"Huh? Wha-?" You sat up, still groggy from lack of sleep. Why were you so tired? Oh, that was right. You'd spent your night fantasizing about your coworker: the very same one that was now eyeing you in your sleeping shirt. It buttoned down the front, but you had left it open near the collar after last night's ministrations with your hands and toy. Not that you could pay attention to the expanse of cleavage you were revealing, as your recently developed crush was currently occupying your senses.

Doran had entered your room dressed in a baseball uniform. The uniform was tight against his lean muscles, the high socks hugging his calves and the pants just situated to reveal the sweet curvature of his ass. His hat was on backwards, set atop his messy auburn hair.

"Am I dreaming?" your hands roamed over your flushed face. You hadn't thought of this one yet, but you wouldn't put it past yourself.

"Oh! Oh, no Ms. _____," Doran looked out the window with a blush. "I didn't mean to walk in on you sleeping, I just thought you were up and all. It's almost time for breakfast."

"Breakfast," you blinked. Man, you were bad at getting up early. It was one of the things you'd struggled with as a teacher. Hearing Doran calling you Miss as he stood embarrassed in his baseball uniform had your brain spinning down a whole different track. You couldn't help but want to make this grown man your teacher's pet.

You smiled in embarrassment. "Don't worry Doran," you kicked your feet out of bed, "I'll get ready fast." His eyes followed you as you walked to your dresser. You turned towards him; your hair was disheveled from sleep. "Should I- um- do I have a uniform to wear today?"

"What?" You could see his eyes quickly leave your backside: not so innocent after all. *Was he interested?* You had thought it was just his personality to be so friendly with you the night before, but now you were gaining perspective. "No!" He blushed, "No, Ms. _____. I just wore this because it's Baseball Day. I thought it might get the campers excited."

"Uh-huh," you gave him elevator eyes because you felt his comment and observations had given you consent. He looked so damn cute you had to stop yourself from biting your lip. "So, I'll just put on my regular t-shirt and shorts. And Doran?"

"Y-yes?" his voice hiked as his expression grew concerned.

"You don't have to call me Miss. I mean- unless you want to."

"Yes, Ms._____. I mean," he struggled, "of course, _____."

You opened your drawer as he continued watching. "Would you- ?" you stalled.

"Oh, right!" He stepped backwards towards the door, "Where is my mind today? I- uh- I'll just be outside."

You grinned, "Thanks Doran. I'll be out in a sec."

She's so beautiful! Doran thought to himself as his back collapsed against the side of your cabin. He closed his eyes. Many more days like this and he wouldn't be able to control himself. He hadn't relieved these feelings last night, perhaps that was why he was feeling so strongly about you today. Either that or maybe- just maybe- something was different.

He didn't want to sound conceited or anything, but something was new in the way that you looked at him. And he was looking at you too. Your soft curves, your feminine frame. Guilt mingled with lust as he took a deep breath and tried to count backwards from ten. Could it somehow be possible that you felt this way when you were around him? You just seemed so confident; he couldn't tell.

He cursed his inability to hide his emotions. He always wore them on his sleeve. Although, he internally patted himself on the back for not declaring his desire for you in your bedroom. His duty to you as his co-counselor came first. It should always come first no matter how strongly he felt. No matter how much his heart climbed in his throat and his head swam.

"Ready, Doran?" your clothes were normal, but you wore an old cap backwards to suit his style.

His smile grew exponentially at the sight. "Let's play ball!"

Chapter Four: Rewards

Baseball Day was fun. Although it was something more of a Wiffle Ball Day. Several balls were dredged from the bottom of Lake Sumac, at the center of the camp. You had learned not to expect much in the way of supplies by now, since Z wasn't much of a spender. Yet Doran treated the day as if it was the World Series. His enthusiasm had a positive effect on you, and you hoped that it trickled down to the campers. Some were more easily influenced than others. To your surprise, Billy was doing an excellent job as umpire. That much could be seen when conflict arose on the field.

"I saw that!" Amy cried out. "You've been throwing the ball so that Josh can't hit it!"

"Yeah, Blake," Jessie flipped some hair out of her eyes, "Josh is normally awesome at this, but the ball just keeps curving out of range."

"Guys, you know I suck at sports, right?" Josh interceded.

Blake, the camp jock, crossed his arms. "Maybe Josh just can't hit it."

"You take that back!" Aisha growled, "He can hit any curve ball any day!"

Suddenly everyone was contributing their two cents and crowding the sandlot.

"People, people!" Billy raised his hands. "We can settle this by having a rotation of pitchers. Aisha, since you are obviously on Josh's side- even though you are on the opposite team- you can pitch. Throw a curveball, and then we can see if Josh can hit it."

Aisha threw a pitch, which was hardly a curveball, and Josh bunted it. The campers saw it wasn't a tricky hit and shrugged off Blake's pitching as a fluke. After a few more hits and rotations it didn't matter anyway; the campers appeared to be having fun.

"Great job resolving conflict, Billy!" Doran complimented as he clasped him on the back. "Let's see what reward you wrote on your card." Doran shuffled through his green deck. "Aha!" Doran read aloud the first choice, "Billy wants to go to Pizzaville," he looked up, "to have a pizza party."

The crowd of kids buzzed and squealed; some pumped their fists. Jessie gave a smirk.

"To town?" Doran looked up from the card. Billy nodded.

"This would involve travel and reservations." Doran winced, "Maybe we could have one at the camp?"

Billy's face grew hard, "No fair. You were the one who wanted this system."

"He's right," said Jessie. "You need to fulfill your promises if you want people to trust you."

The kids began grumbling in agreement as you counselors exchanged glances. "Come on Doran," Atticus spoke up, "We've got an old school bus and we've got another counselor now. We can keep track of everybody."

"The bus," Doran dropped his fist into his hand as if he'd forgotten. "Right. Yes. I think this can work. Everybody should get ready; we're heading out in thirty minutes! _____, you call the restaurant and tell them we're on our way."

"Got it!"

The kids were loaded onto the bus and double counted. Triple counted with Doran's personal review. You noticed that Jessie had taken a seat in the back and smiled to yourself at the perceived coolness of the action. All the counselors were up front. "All right, we're ready!" Doran walked up the row towards the driver's seat as the sun fell lower in the sky.

Z then moved Doran aside. "I've got this. If there's pizza, I want some, too."

"Oh, right. Lead the way." Doran leaned over your seat as Z got adjusted in the small space. Your seat was for two people. Doran's long arms stretched over to the window, and the seat backing behind you, as his knee rested its weight between your legs. You couldn't help but feel surrounded. You had admired the baseball uniform but were glad to see him back in counselor attire. And his shorts afforded you the pleasure of feeling the heat from his leg next to your thigh in the sticky summer heat.

"Oh, hi _____," he smiled with a blush.

"Hi Doran," your eyes searched his face as the engine started.

"Look!" Doran leaned absent-mindedly closer to you as he pointed out the window, "Wow, what beautiful sunset."

You sat up in your seat and struggled to look away from his shining face. "It really is. Thank you for sharing it with me."

"My pleasure," he looked at you for a moment before realizing his circumstances. Doran swiftly pulled back and took a seat at your side. As he looked away from you, out the opposite window, he began to softly sing a tune to a traveling song. You recognized it from your childhood at a different camp. Although the words were probably incorrect, you sang along, and the rest of the bus was subjected to a musical spectacle they wanted no part in.

Pizzaville was a homey little restaurant; it reminded you of one you'd once worked at as a teenager. You were glad to be out of the service industry. Although you wondered if what you were doing now could be called some sort of service. The kids took up the whole restaurant. They were crowded by fours into different booths and tables. Only the counselors and the handyman were left standing.

Doran was mingling among the tables. He was still trying to initiate a conversation with Jessie, which was going nowhere. *Let her come to you, Doran.* You sighed with a smile. The girl may not have been old enough to realize what a great older brother she had. Maybe she was embarrassed and didn't want her friends to know about her homelife.

"Hey," Atticus whispered, "_____!"

"Hm?" You looked back to see a red solo cup in his hand. Z was sipping from a bottle, his back against the serving bar.

Atticus spoke behind his hand into your ear, "this place has beer!"

After a long day and a sleepless night, it would be nice to have one. Still, "I don't know."

"What? You're old enough, aren't ya?" Z asked.

You laughed. "I've been over twenty-one for a while now."

At that, he pushed a cup your way. "Here, it's on me. You've earned it."

"Oh, okay." You looked down at the frothy drink. "Sure. Why not?"

"Hey, Doran." Jessie stuffed her face with a slice.

"Yes, Jessie?" the counselor turned around.

"How come you're the only one of the counselors without a red cup? You don't drink or something?"

Doran's mouth dropped as he observed you and Atticus before turning back to Jessie. "Nice try. They're drinking soda."

"Sure," Jessie nodded, "soda- if that's what they're calling it these days. Hey, _____!" she called.

You looked over and squinted your eyes at the situation. Doran looked a little pale. But the drink had lowered your guard. You could handle it. You swallowed the last of it and recycled your cup. "Yes, Jessie?"

Jessie grinned. "Tell me something about biology."

Your face lit up, "Really?"

"Oh yeah. Go wild."

Your words blended together, "ThebiologicaldiversityofCampOakisquiteimpreesive!I'veseenavast arrayoffloraandfauna.Didyouknowthatevolutionarily-"

"Okay!" Jessie held up her hand. "I settle my case."

"She just-" Doran looked between you two, "It's her subject." He turned to you, "_____, can I have a word with you?"

"Of course," you smiled as Doran gently took you by the arm and walked you outside. On the side of the building, you placed your head on the cool brick wall. That felt good.

"Were you drinking alcohol?" Doran's brow raised.

"No," you pressed yourself further against the wall, "I mean, yes?"

"You were?" He observed you with a look of worry.

"Is that against the rules?" You stumbled, "I mean, Atticus and Z were-"

Doran looked down at the sidewalk.

"Doran?" you shrunk a little.

"My mother was a drinker-" he breathed, "I don't drink much. It just leaves me with an uneasy feeling: adults drinking around kids." He looked up. "One of the conditions to be a counselor at Camp Oak is to stay sober on the job."

"I'm sorry, I didn't know. It must have been in the fine print of the contract." You reached into your pocket. "Here, you can choose one of my punishments."

He looked down at the red card and back at your face. He seemed so far away.

"Go on," you opened his fist and put your card in his palm. "You can punish me."

"...Me?" He looked at you.

With a shared vulnerability, you nodded.

"Well, then," he looked at your card then his eyes flickered over your face. "I guess you'll be cleaning the mess hall when we get back."

"I will, and I won't drink on the job again. Does that make you feel better?"

Doran nodded. "I guess it does."

"Good. Me too. So, what do we do about Atticus and Z?"

Doran's mouth turned into a thin line, "I don't think anybody *could* do something about Z. He's not really a counselor anyway. Atticus, on the other hand, will be missing out on his podcast for the rest of the week."

You would have thought the carbs from the pizza and soda would have wound everyone up, but the day spent out in the sun and a night of fun had most campers passed out on the ride home.

Aisha was curled up and Josh had his head back, mouth open in a silent snore. You marveled at Jessie's sleeping face. She had to use so many muscles to frown and scowl. Now there was an air of peace about her that you hated to interrupt. "Hey," you whispered to the group, "it's time to go to bed. We're home."

"Home?!" Jessie sat up swiftly with a look of confused apprehension. "Oh no," she held her head, "I'm still here with the drunk lady who talks too much."

"I am *not* drunk," you scrunched up your face. "After that ride I'm happy to say I'm completely sober. What did you have to go and rat me out for anyway?"

She smiled easily at you, "Relax, Teach. I wanted to see Doran get angry at someone his own size. Seemed dignified though, he took you outside." She paused as if remembering something in a cold sweat. "He didn't hit you, did he?"

"What... Doran? No. He wouldn't do that."

She shrugged. "You never know."

You'd take note of that statement. "So, you want to get rid of me that bad, eh?"

"Not particularly." She looked out the window. "You've still got a job to do."

"That's right: to see if the soft man cares. Come on Jessie, isn't it obvious that he does?"

"Ignore the obvious," Jessie looked at you keenly. "Look at what's underneath. Understand why he acts like an idiot. What's his motive?"

"Okay, Jessie. Whatever you say. You know, you're starting to sound like a scientist. Do you have a hypothesis?"

"Josh," Jessie elbowed her friend awake, "she's using your words again."

It was nine in the evening and the campers had all been sent to bed, yet you stood in the cafeteria with a mop and bucket.

Z gestured, "Thanks for helping with the floors and latrines. Looks like you're gunning for my job. Should I be concerned?"

"Not at all; this sweet gig's all yours."

"Or maybe you're just gunning for me?" He raised a brow playfully.

"Har. Har." You leaned against the mop handle. "You know Z, you were drinking too. Shouldn't you be punished?"

You could see the corners of his cheeks lift from under his mustache. "Wanna punish me?"

"Um," you straightened your back. "Yeah! Yeah, I do. You gave me the beer in the first place."

He looked you over as if contemplating something. "Come to the dock at midnight."

"Elaborate?" You had no idea what he was talking about.

"You'll see," he winked as he walked away.

Doran walked past the man and the two exchanged a glance as Z walked out the door. Doran looked as if he wasn't expecting that. "Um, okay. Co-counselor _____, I'll be here overseeing your punishment."

"But, Doran, it's late." You began mopping, "Isn't that like punishing yourself?"

"Not really, it gives me more time to get to know you."

"Well, that's nice." You swept under the table. "I guess I could get to know you better as well. Go ahead and ask a question."

"Hm. How did you get into biology?"

"Easy. I was always climbing trees as a kid. And as I grew up, I wanted to know more about them. I lived near the woods, so nature was close and full of new life to explore. There are so many different organisms. So many things to know; it's fascinating."

"I know what you mean," Doran spoke fondly.

"I hope you don't mind, but can I ask something a camper would like to ask you?"

Doran sat up on the table. "A camper? Why wouldn't they ask me?"

"When I ask, I think you'll know."

"Oh, okay… Ask away."

"Do you genuinely care about the people at this camp?"

"What?" Doran stood to stand beside you, "_____, of course I do."

"I know, Doran." You smiled up at him. "This particular one thinks you're too good to be true. Or can't understand why you aren't as miserable as the rest of the world."

"I think I know who you're talking about." Doran looked down and away. "Jessie has the same notion that I had as a kid: adults don't care. When I grew up, my parents were never there. I acted out as a because of that. I latched on to any mentors I could find. Even if they weren't the greatest." His eyes grew wet as he looked out the window into the black night.

"Oh, Doran…" You abandoned your mop to sit beside him at the table. "Is it okay if I-?"

"Of course." He opened his palm in answer to your unspoken question and held your hand as he spoke. "I ignored their flaws because I wanted to believe the world was a better place. And I was acting permissive with the kids because, well… Because of what I lacked. I wasn't given anything as a kid, so I wanted to give them everything. I still do. But I know now that there have to be boundaries to show that I care. This camp is my family, just as Jessie is my family." He looked up to you with a wilted expression. "*Of course*, I care. I probably annoy Jessie because she's the one that needs to be cared about the most."

Without thinking, you wrapped your arms around his neck and back.

"_____?" He questioned. "Are you upset? I'm sorry, I didn't mean to... I won't punish you anymore!"

"Idiot," you breathed against his throat, "you're the one that needs to be cared about the most. At least as Jessie's brother, you're there for her. If you don't feel like anyone's there for you, I want you to know that I'm there. I care about you, Doran."

"You do?" He looked down at your body pressed against his.

"I do. Very much." You pulled back, feeling slightly awkward. "I'll be here to remind you whenever you need me."

"Thank you, _____." He smiled. "I care about you too."

Your heart whelmed and you suddenly felt shy. "I should probably get back to cleaning." You stood to go.

"Wait," he caught your wrist, "I think that's enough for tonight. Let's get some rest." "Thank you," you beamed. "I should put the supplies away though."

Doran grabbed the mop and bucket as you carried the cleaning fluid.

Chapter Five: Renew

"Doran?" you asked as you placed the cleaning fluid back on the shelf.

He organized the mop and bucket near the sink behind you. "Yes?"

"Have you ever been to the dock at midnight?"

He was silent for a moment, and you had to turn around to make sure he was still there.

"No!" His voice was strangled, "I'd never go there. Not now, at least."

"What's the matter?" you played, "Are you scared?"

"_____!" His face grew red. "I don't know if you have any idea what you're talking about! That's more of Zephan's kind of thing."

"Well, I don't know. It could be your kind of thing, too."

He looked at you with his mouth open, eyes searching yours in the confining closet. "Are you... into that?"

You squinted, "Wait. Are we talking about the same thing here?"

"Don't make me say it," he shook his head.

"He just asked me to meet him there. I don't know what it means."

Doran slowly sat against the cabinet.

"You look so pale, are you all right?" You knelt beside him and took some animal crackers from storage. "Do you need something to eat?"

Doran suddenly wrapped his arms around you. "_____," his voice quavered, "you promise me you'll never go there at midnight, all right? You take care of yourself. Don't let anybody lay a finger on you."

"Oh, okay Doran… Can I ask why?" You sat beside him and placed your hand in his waiting palm. It seemed like he'd been touch starved for a while, and he was growing accustomed to the feeling of your skin on his. His fingers gave you a comfortably tight squeeze.

"That was highly inappropriate of him to ask you. After all, you couldn't have consented if you didn't know what he was talking about." He looked back at you pleadingly, "*Do* you know?"

You shook your head.

"It's a-" he paused as you saw a dusting of red return to his features. "It's a sex thing," he whispered.

"No!" Your eyes grew wide, "Really?"

"Really." Doran nodded. "Him and some people from town meet at the dock and ride a boat into the woods for some pagan fun, if you know what I mean."

You were inquisitive, "An orgy? Have you ever seen it?"

"No! Never! I haven't even-" his voice trailed off.

"Oh," you understood, but your curiosity begged you to go farther. "If you don't mind me asking, how far would you say that you…"

Doran looked at you for a moment. Then he looked down. "If I tell you, will you tell me too?"

"Sure," you held out your pinky, "it'll be our shared secret." You wrapped them in the form of a promise.

"I've done it," Doran spoke quietly, "but not all the way."

You marveled at this handsome wholesome creature before you. "You didn't want to go any farther?"

"I did," he bit his lip, "but I got anxious. I start thinking this person is going to leave me or not think I'm so great, and I end up making it awkward. I'm pretty hopeless at love."

"Oh, Doran." You held his hand tighter. "I think you'd be great at love. You just haven't found the right person yet."

"Thank you," he smiled. "Would it be all right if I asked about your…"

"I've been intimate," you felt yourself flush as you said it. "But… I've never been truly in love with somebody."

"Oh," he spoke.

You wondered if he hated you yet.

"What do you think it would take for you to fall in love?"

That was his first question? You laughed, "I'm not sure. When you know, you know, right?"

"Right," he nodded.

"Would it help… if someone were to love you first?"

You looked into his eyes and found it to be a serious question. "Perhaps," you spoke as you examined his lips. "I think the best way to tell if you can love somebody is the feeling you get when you kiss."

He looked at you softly, "May I… kiss you?"

You responded with action, laying a chaste kiss on his accepting lips. You pulled back to examine his expression and saw a hunger there you'd never seen before. Suddenly, his hands were in your hair, holding you in place as his mouth was on your own; his tongue licked your lower lip. Soon, you were lost in an undulating series of soft and rough kisses. You both pulled back and examined each other's heated faces.

Doran suddenly became aware of his surroundings. "I'm- I'm sorry!" he scrambled. "You're my coworker, I never should have-"

"Doran, we're both consenting adults. There's no law against having a thing for or with your co-counselor."

39

"But we work together! What if you get tired of me? What if you don't like-"

"Doran, you're self-sabotaging. It's okay if two people don't like each other anymore. It's okay if two people do. If things don't work out, we will be amicable." You thought for a moment, "We won't let anyone else know if that makes you feel better. That way it'll be like nothing's changed."

He looked at you curiously, "So, that's how you deal with a breakup if you're not in love?"

"I guess so." You shrugged.

"Wow," he looked down, "I'd cry for days."

"Doran," you smiled as you cupped his face, "there's about one month left in the summer. I can honestly say that I won't get tired of you."

"Do you promise?" His eyes were hopeful.

"I promise. Hey, even if things don't work out, you're a great guy. I'll be your friend for as long as you let me." You put your other hand on his chest, "I'll be here."

He wrapped his hand around yours with a half-smile. "I believe you."

"It's Swimming Day!" Doran burst into your room a few days later. He'd asked you before if you minded his intrusion, and you'd told him truthfully you didn't. It wasn't bad to wake up to a song of good morning as he flipped the blinds open to let in the early sunlight.

"Mm. Good morning." You rolled over and rubbed your eyes. When you opened them you felt like rubbing them once more.

Doran stood before you in lifeguard shorts with a white line across on his nose; aviators were perched on his head behind a wave of hair. His chest was bare, with a whistle around it that directed you towards the sparse hair that trailed into his shorts. On his lean muscled body, his abs were his best feature.

"Come here," You knelt on the bed in your matching pajama set and beckoned him over. "_____?" He questioned as he walked forward, "What is it? Are you sick?"

"No," you smiled, "I just wanted to see you."

"Oh," he stood by your bedside.

"May I touch you?" You looked into his eyes.

"Y-yeah," he blushed.

"Here?" You questioned as you pointed to his stomach.

He nodded warily.

You placed your warm hand on him tentatively, brushing it up and down: like a washboard.

"_____!" he laughed. "That tickles."

"Sorry," you grinned, satisfied with your explorations for now. "Once again, I have to ask. Should I be wearing a swimsuit or-"

"Of course! Today we're going into Lake Sumac to test the kids' swimming levels."

"I'm guessing you're a certified lifeguard with those shorts?"

"Someone's got to keep Camp Oak safe," he smiled.

"And what would you do if there was a shark?"

"Shark? There are no sharks in-"

"Shark attack!" You called as you wrapped your arms around him and pulled him onto your bed.

"Ah!" he yelped in surprise as you nipped him lightly with your mouth and hands.

"_____," he laughed as he curled up, "_____!"

You pulled back and smiled at him flush and grinning on your bed. "You're so handsome," slipped from your mouth.

His smile faded as his eyes became more thoughtful.

"Come on," you suggested, "we've got some kids to train."

"Maybe I should teach you mouth to mouth first," he said quietly.

"Oh! You're sly," you looked back at his wide smile. "Okay. You can step out now, while I change."

"Aw," Doran mock complained as you pushed him out and closed the door.

You looked down at the bikini you had brought. You hadn't figured you'd be the one swimming at camp. And if you were, you thought it would be adult swim. You sighed, it wasn't like it was too revealing or anything. It was probably what the kids' moms would wear anyway: something simple and black. It would have to do.

"What do you think?" You asked as you stepped out in your new suit.

Doran's cheeks grew red, "Beautiful."

"Thanks Doran," you felt butterflies when you caught him glimpsing as you walked towards the lake.

Needless to say, you felt a little awkward in your bikini in front of the kids. But that feeling slowly went away as you submerged yourself in the murky water. You were hanging near the edge of the dock, working on treading water. Since you weren't an expert like Doran or experienced like Atticus, your group did not consist of the best swimmers in the bunch. It consisted of Amy, Josh, and Billy.

"Ms. _____! Ms. _____!"

You looked up on the dock, "Yes, Aisha?"

"I can do a cannonball, watch!"

"Aisha!" Atticus called from the shoreline, "Their time isn't up yet, we aren't diving from the dock for another five minutes."

The girl squealed as she leapt from the platform.

"Aisha!" Doran called from deeper in the water, "Watch out for the other campers!"

You observed in slow motion as she dove on top of smaller Amy, bringing her under in a tidal splash. You had worked with her on holding her breath underwater and found that she wasn't great at it. *Oh crap.* You instinctively went under. Struggling to see in the murky water, you felt through rocks and aquatic plants. You swam further towards the bottom and grabbed Amy's arm. Aisha was treading water above you. Her foot caught your suit, and something snapped. You didn't have time to think about it as you brought Amy to the surface. You took a breath; she took a breath.

Doran took a breath. "I'm so glad you're both okay!" he spoke from under his wet locks. They draped over his eyes with the added weight. He brushed them back. Then he took a breath as if he were the one afraid of drowning.

"What?" You looked at him. "Doran?"

Doran looked down at your top, which while still attached around your neck was disconnected at the back. You followed his gaze and felt around for the plastic clasp. It was gone. "Aisha must have caught it with her foot," you spoke under your breath as you relinquished Amy to the dock.

"I held my breath; did you see me?"

"Good job, Amy!" you smiled. She didn't swallow any water so she should be okay.

"It's going to be all right," Doran's voice assured you as he held the torn pieces together behind your back.

"It's okay, kids! _____ just twisted her ankle and needs some first aid. Atticus, I think we're through with swimming for the day."

Everyone groaned as they began to pull themselves out of the water.

"Aisha," Doran's face was stern, "that was a dangerous thing to do. I want to see your red card when we get back."

"Aw, man." She splashed the water in disappointment. "Sorry, Ms. _____!"

"It's okay, Aisha." You spoke as you waded to land. "It was a good cannonball. Just not on Amy." You walked with David back to your cabin as the kids headed to the showers to prepare for the rest of the day.

"Thanks Doran," you sighed when you were both inside and the door was locked. "That could have been really awkward."

"No problem, _____. Should I...'" He swallowed, "Should I let go now?"

You looked into his shy and curious eyes, "Yes, you can let go."

He did so slowly, removing his warm hand and allowing the cold fabric to slide across your skin. He looked down, "I'll go wait outside."

You tilted his chin up with your index finger, "No, I think you can stay."

"I can?"

"Do you want to?"

"Yes," he breathed.

You removed your top, without giving him time to second guess.

"_____!" He blushed as he struggled to keep his gaze level with yours.

"It's okay," you encouraged, "you can look."

He looked from one breast to the other, as if he couldn't decide which his favorite was. Then he gazed up at you, asking if it was all right.

"Would you like to touch them?"

He bit his lip and nodded before ghosting his hands over your flesh. You melted into his delicate touch.

"Is this all right?" Doran worried, "My ex said I was never rough enough. I think she dumped me over it."

"Doran," you placed your hand on top of his, "your ex was an idiot. This feels amazing."

He smiled as his thumbs rubbed circles on your nipples; his index finger slowly moved back and forth, teasing you sweetly. "You're beautiful," he spoke against your pebbled skin, which was still cold from the lake.

"Should I take these off too?" You ran your thumb under the tied waist of your bottoms.

"I- um," he stalled. "You have to change into counselor attire anyway."

"You're right," you cooed as you slipped your swimsuit off. As it hit the floor, you could see his excitement evident through his swim trunks. "Do you like what you see?"

His eyes softened. "Very much."

"I like what I see too," you trailed your fingers towards his waistband and looked to him for guidance. He nodded as you slipped your hand into his damp shorts and wrapped it around the heated length of him. He gasped as his eyes closed and his hips jerked forward. He would fit you perfectly.

"You feel so good in my hand," you hummed.

"It feels so good, _____," he cupped your face as his eyes glazed, "I want to kiss you."

You did as he wanted, toying with him as his lips tasted yours. He'd lost focus on playing with your chest, but you didn't mind. That meant he was enjoying things. You could tell that it wouldn't be long if you… "Can I use my mouth?"

His face went beet red, and he bit his lip. Still, he nodded just the same.

You pulled down his swim trunks, revealing exactly what you wanted to see. You looked up at him quivering above you as you licked him tentatively. He twitched before you wrapped your

45

mouth around him. His skin was still slightly cold from the lake water.

He gasped as his eyes shut tight, "Ah!" his hips moved inadvertently as you worked him into a frenzied state. His hand tapped you politely on the shoulder. "I'm going to... I'm... I'm going to..."

You stayed as you received everything he had to offer. "_____!" he called out your name as he came. When you removed yourself he slumped to the floor beside you. "Wow," he breathed, "thank you."

"You're welcome," You wiped your mouth with the back of your hand and gave him a kiss. "Now. Let's get changed and head back to camp."

"Camp!" His face became a whole new shade of red at the realization.

Jessie watched as the two of you exited your cabin. You were in your counselor attire and Doran still in his swimsuit as he headed to change in his own space. He had a dopey smile on his face. The middle schooler's eyes became wide with understanding and then narrowed again. "So, Doran gets lunch and a show," Jessie commented.

Your heart sped up. "What do you mean?"

"That's not what you were wearing when you went into your cabin, but it was when you came out. Doran was still in his swim shorts. Logic says: he saw you change."

Your mouth became a thin line as you thought of possible retorts. *Should you lie? Should you tell the truth about your relationship?* If this kid had any leverage on you, she would milk it for all it was worth. So, you decided to offer a question rather than an answer. "What if I changed first and Doran was just checking up on me after waiting outside? That's another possibility."

"It's a possibility," Jessie walked around you, assessing you for weak points. "It's also possible that I'm the next president of the United States."

You both had a smirk on your faces.

"Listen," Jessie crossed her arms. "Doran may be annoying- and about as gullible as a baby dropped on its head- but don't use him to figure out the truth to our bet. That's not fair."

"Use him?" You squinted.

"Emotional extortion. I don't want to wade through a river of his snot and tears again."

"...Again?"

"What are you, a parrot?" Jessie sneered, "He had his heart broken last summer."

"That's awful!"

Jessie looked you up and down. "Yeah. The guy doesn't have much luck with dating apps."

"Geez..." You had to laugh at such an innocent, well-mannered guy trying to navigate through those murky waters. You knew he wasn't going to find what he was looking for that way. But something in you felt a little eaten away.

"Yeah," Jessie harrumphed, "so don't mess around."

"Aw, Jessie," you cooed, "does that mean you care about me- or that you care about Doran?"

"Shut up. I couldn't care less about you both! I'm just fighting for self-preservation here."

"Jessie," you knelt, "I found the answer to your question, if you would like to hear it."

47

"Wow. You must have some type of body under that baggy t-shirt."

"Don't even go there," you warned, "if you want the truth."

For the first time since her sleeping face you saw her brows relax. "What is it?"

"He cares. He cares about everyone here, kid and adult. Maybe he even cares about you the most. You're like two sides of a coin."

Jessie tilted her head, "Did he tell you why he gives a crap if we smile?"

"He did."

Jessie blinked, "Why?"

"I think you should ask him yourself."

"You're lying!" Jessie's eyes had a sudden fierceness to them. "He didn't tell you anything!"

"It's a personal story Jessie," you tried to soothe her, "I'm sure you wouldn't want me telling yours for you."

"I don't care." She looked down. "I really don't. If we're like two sides of a coin, how could we be so different? I'm not like him. I couldn't be. Even if we are family. How am I supposed to believe that one day I'll wake up with a huge smile on my face? That's never gonna happen! No matter how much he wants it!"

"Oh, Jessie," you swallowed, "I'm sure he doesn't expect that from you. No one does."

"What *does* he want?"

"He just wants you to have a good time; for you to be happy, in your own way. He doesn't want to change who you are. Jessie..." you put a hand on her shoulder as you stood up. "This conversation never happened. If anyone asks you were just telling me how dumb I was for leaving my shoelaces untied."

"What?" she blinked up at you confusedly.

"There are my favorite people!" Doran's cheery voice came towards you as he made his way down the path. His smile suddenly faded as it came to rest on Jessie's teary eyes: tears she refused to ever let fall. "Is everything okay?"

"I was just laughing at this idiot who tripped over her laces." Jessie coughed. "Hah! It was great. Should have seen it. Anyway, see ya."

"Jessie!" Doran called, "Safety is not funny!"

You softly put your hand out to keep Doran from going any further. "Let's let that one go," you smiled, "for now."

Chapter Six: Retreat

"Say, _____?"

"Hm?" You looked up from the book you'd borrowed from Atticus. You had to admit, he had good taste in thrillers. As Doran's softly pleading eyes caught yours over the book, you knew there was something he was struggling to say.

"What is it, Doran?" You gave him your full attention as you laid the novel on the picnic table.

"Atticus did something nice; he said he and Zephan could keep an eye on the campers today. It's Saturday, so they won't be doing planned activities."

"That is nice," you nodded, knowing that wasn't the full statement. "That leaves you free to do lots of things."

"And... you as well." Doran held his arm as he turned to stare at the lake.

It was cute to see him sweat. "Doran," you purred, "are you trying to ask me something?"

He turned, "Would you like to do something with me today? And maybe... tonight?"

"Oh," you swallowed, now you were the one to sweat. It had been a couple of days since your after-swim experience. You weren't exactly sure what Doran's sentiments on the subject were since he was hardly one to talk. But you enjoyed it. Maybe tonight would give you some time to talk? "I'd love to."

"Really?" He sat beside you as you tangled your hand in his.

"You seem excited," you tilted your head curiously. "Do you have something planned, like dinner or a movie? Was there something going on in town?"

"I would love to take you for a hike," Doran's smile was coy and genuine, "and I know a nice spot to camp."

You had to let out a little laugh, "I should have expected that."

"It's in a sheltered redwood grove with some of the largest-"

"Oh!" You grasped his shirt a little too enthusiastically, "Take me!"

His eyes widened, then calmed. "I thought you'd like it. The problem is, I only have one tent." The summer breeze picked up from the lake. He searched your eyes, "Would that be okay?"

You had to look away with a shy smile of your own. "I'd like that." Your eyes flicked up, "But, you'd better have bed rolls or cots! Sleeping on the hard ground is tough."

"Two words:" Doran cupped his hand as his whisper tickled your ear, "inflatable mattress."

"Atticus!" You whined as you filled a backpack with everything you thought you'd need. "Thank you so much for this, but I have no idea what I'm doing!"

He pretty much had you two pegged from the swimming fiasco. Doran was a happy guy, but never that happy. Before you came, camp was a struggle against anarchy. Now, a peaceful routine had settled on Camp Oak and the smile never left Doran's face. "Relax," Atticus kicked his boots onto your desk. "I could walk you through the steps, if this is something you've never done before."

"Quit joking," your brow furrowed.

His dark eyes lingered for a moment too long on yours. "Me? Joke? No way."

"Right."

"The offer still stands."

Maybe if you'd never met Doran. "No thanks."

"All right. Just don't get caught in the act by any machete-wielding murderers. So, I'm guessing you **have** done this before?"

"Yeah," you breathed, "but I have no idea what Doran expects from me."

"Hm," he tapped his chin, "undying love and devotion followed by marriage, a log cabin house, and several legitimate children?"

You always were one to buck at commitment. You'd never been in love. Hell, you couldn't even keep one career for too long!

Atticus took one glance at the frightened look on your face and put his hand on your shoulder. "Woah, woah! You know that I was joking, right? It's Doran. He'll be blissful if you give him prolonged eye contact."

"You're right," you laughed. "I guess it was silly of me to get worked up over an air mattress."

"Oh. Dear. *God.* He brought out the air mattress?" Atticus grasped you, "Don't you break his heart! Do you hear me?!"

You felt a little frazzled as you hiked a fairly worn path shaded by cypress, cedar, and pine. Doran looked to you as the path grew narrower and he had to walk in front. "Everything all right, _____?"

"Yeah…" you nodded. You weren't exactly sure where this was going: the path or the relationship. You were afraid of commitment. But you were even more afraid of breaking Doran's heart.

"It's okay." His hand interrupted your thoughts as it grasped yours; his thumb rubbed soothing circles. "I sometimes feel lost at the start of an adventure, too."

You looked up to his sea green eyes and found your center. "You're right," you smiled. "Everything will be okay."

You stopped to have lunch on an outcropping that overlooked the mountains and valleys. The rivers were blue satin below, catching the sunlight. Birds circled above in the clear cerulean sky. The day was dry and warm with a light breeze. As you sat on the cool stone, Doran handed you some sliced apples.

"This is really sweet of you Doran, thank you."

"I'm happy to share." He smiled as you finished your snack. "Come on," he put out his hand, pulling you up with more strength than you could visibly see. It caused you to stumble, but he held you fast on the rocks. There was safety there, a trust in those arms that you'd never known. Despite what you had done sexually, you found yourself blushing like a schoolgirl. "Sorry." He helped you stand. "Seems I don't know my own strength." He stepped away. "I still want to show you the redwoods and set up camp before dark. The journey downhill should be easier than the one that got us here."

You smiled as you followed the man in front of you. How was it that his lithe body held such strength, such optimism, and such passion? It was a mystery. But you were thankful for the handsome package that it came in. Doran held your hand to guide you over the rocks. After sidestepping down a few steep declines and observing the change in flora, you knew you were close to the campsite. The soil was drier, almost sandy. Then, you heard it. "A river!" You called out.

"I hear it, too," he beamed back at you. "This river is one that we viewed at lunch. It looks so tiny from up there, but it's much larger down here. It'll be nice to camp by, since moving water keeps the mosquitos away."

"What a luxury!"

He laughed and turned to you in the clearing. "Here we are."

"Wow," you looked around. Wildflowers were scattered in the meadow beyond the towering redwoods. The air smelled of pine and honey. You admired the view as you set up the tent and gathered firewood. Doran blew up the air mattress with a small motor that rattled along with your heart. It was much darker here in the valley. The trees blocked out the setting sun.

Doran smiled, "Come with me! There's still one thing I want you to see before it gets dark."

You giggled, "Sure," as the two of you sped, hand in hand, over the flat terrain.

Then, Doran took a step out in front of you. "Close your eyes." You followed suit and closed them, feeling the broadness of Doran's warm hands sweep over you. He turned you around with a gentle ease. "Now look."

You blinked as the warmth left your face. "A petrified redwood!" You gasped in awe at the rainbow-colored stump before you. It looked like a forest jewel.

"You've got it! I knew you would, Ms. _____. It's been around since the dinosaurs."

"Amazing!" You walked around the stump, checking it out from all angles.

"Do you like it?" His voice was soft.

"Doran, I love it!" You grabbed him and kissed him sweetly.

He looked at your face, lost for a moment before he pulled you closer, deepening the kiss and sending shivers up your spine.

"Let's head back to the campsite," you encouraged, "we should get a fire going for dinner."

"You're right," Doran looked up at the sky. "Come on. It's not far."

You walked back to the clearing together as the sounds of the forest at night came forth.

"I never thought I'd meet anyone like you," Doran spoke as his striker lit the kindling with ease.

"I never thought I'd meet anyone like you either," you echoed as you stared into the dancing flames; they reminded you of the night when he'd first reached out to hold you. "But I'm so glad I did."

"So am I," Doran nodded. "I wish I had my guitar so I could show you how much."

"Doran," you grinned, "you don't need a guitar."

"No?"

"Doran," you placed your hand over his, "if you romance me anymore I'll die. You know that I already want you, right?"

"You... do?" his eyes searched yours.

"I do."

"...Why?" His expression was vulnerable.

"Because of everything that you are."

He breathed in realization as he nervously ran a hand through his hair. "Did you ever feel like everything's going too well? Like the world will open up at any second?"

"It's all right," you responded in the same manner he had before, tracing circles on his hand. "We're not a part of the world tonight. We can do whatever you want while we're here."

"Well," he looked up with a hunger in his eyes, "there is one thing I'd like to do."

"What's that?" your heart skipped.

"I never got to repay you for your kindness the other day."

You chewed your lip in anticipation as he set you on the mattress. Between kisses, he was stripping you with such eagerness you thought he would eat you whole. But his eagerness mirrored your own.

You'd only gotten him down to his boxer briefs and you were dying to see all of him. The way they cupped his ass and package was making you weak. The light of the fire cast through the opening of the tent, allowing you to admire scattered freckles brought forth from years in the sun. He had some scars, you'd noticed; from years of dealing with tough terrain, you'd hoped.

"You're beautiful," he marveled once more, tracing you with the delicacy you remembered.

"You're handsome," you ran a hand through his wavy hair. It was a soft copper in the firelight.

He leaned into your touch. "I want to taste you."

"Here?" you smiled, hooking your thumbs under your waistband.

"Yes," he breathed.

With a tug, your panties came off.

He gave a light sound of pleasure at the sight. Within seconds, he was on his knees on the tent floor kissing the inside of your thighs. The fire moved behind him, casting shadows of warmth. Then, his lips contacted your clit. You gasped as he kissed it slowly, working his way down and back up again. His tongue came out in uncertain licks, looking to you for guidance. "Just like that," you cooed as he circled you in just the right spot. "Suck on it. Yes! Right there..." You hummed as he did as he was asked, making your leg quiver.

He spoke against you, "You make me so hard."

"Mm. What do you want to do?"

56

"I-It doesn't matter," he blushed.

"It does," you encouraged, "tell me."

His eyes sought yours, "I want to be inside of you."

"Then, take me," you kissed him lightly, "I'm yours."

"You mean it?"

"Please."

"Because I wouldn't mind if you-"

You took the initiative of kissing him deeper so he wouldn't get lost in his head. You rolled him over from his spot at the edge of the bed, reached under his boxers and stroked him slowly until he was gasping for air. "Do you want this, Doran?" You spoke against his lips as you held him in your hand. You could feel him pulsing, bucking against your grip.

He whimpered in response, "Yes, please..."

That was all you needed to hear as you reached in your bag and thanked your lucky stars you were prepared for a summer romance. You held the condom up cautiously.

He nodded.

You lightly trailed your fingers up and down his length as he kicked his boxers from his legs. "Is it okay if I put this on you?"

"Yeah." His face was the color of beets, whether it was from embarrassment or exertion you didn't know.

You took your fingers off him for a moment. "Doran, is it okay if we go this far? Is this how you wanted it to go?"

"It's everything I wanted it to be. Please, you're all I want." His eyes were wet in the firelight.

Your heart filled as you devoured him in a kiss. "I want you," you rolled the condom on with ease, "to take me any way you like." He settled himself on his knees between your legs. His dick slid back and forth on your clit as he looked up to you for assurance. You bucked into him and gave him a show. "Yes, right there. Just like that. I want you inside of me. I need you."

He pressed forward into your slickness as his girth stretched you just right. You gasped as you arched up into him. "That feels good. Does it feel good for you?"

"Ah," he breathed, "yes… So good."

"Good," you smiled. "Don't stop." Slowly, he moved in and out of you. His heated thighs met with the backs of yours. You traced lazy circles around your clit as he did so, causing sparks to emerge in your core. "Yes," you encouraged, "more, faster…"

His breath was heavy as he did so, looking down at you all the while. You were lost in his eyes, lost in the feelings he brought to your body. He kissed you deeply, interrupted by his breathy moans. "So good." His body moved quicker as he supplied much needed pressure over and over again. You were on the edge yourself.

"_____," his breath caught, "I think I'm going to, oh, fuck…"

It was probably that pitched curse word leaving Doran's innocent mouth that did it for you as you both spiraled into orgasm. You held him tight to you as your bodies got lost in one another. His weight was upon you, but it was comfortable, not heavy at all. "I love you, _____," he whispered from somewhere within your hair. Your body lay still; your nerves were still humming. Your mind was drawing a blank as he held you impossibly tighter. "It doesn't matter if you don't feel the same way. I don't expect you to. But, with all of me… I really do." And he let go.

Chapter Seven: Responsible

It seemed the sun rose too soon. After the events of a blissful evening, you returned to the reality that was Camp Oak. The night had left you with more to think about than you'd prepared for when applying to work at a summer camp. *He had said he **loved** you.* It wasn't the first time you'd heard someone say it, but, perhaps, it was the first time you'd believed it. He hadn't expected you to say it in return. You both knew that. And you were thankful that he hadn't imposed such pressure on you. Still, you were feeling a roiling in yourself as you watched him staring out at the lake from atop a splintered picnic table.

"Nice job, dingus," Jessie walked up behind you with her hands on her hips. "The guy can't even remember to cry. What'd you do? Tell him you hate him more than you hate s'mores and sunshine?"

"Nothing like that," you crossed your arms over your chest. You did not want to have this conversation with a child. And especially not a member of his family.

Jessie stared at you for a while. She squinted. Then her eyes grew wide. "You don't love him, do you?"

You looked towards the lake as well. "That's none of your business, Jessie."

"No," Jessie impeded your view. "You just don't want to be responsible."

"I'm very responsible!" Too late you realized you had taken her bait.

"Are you?" Jessie smirked. "You sure don't seem like you want to be held responsible for soft boy's feelings over there."

"We're adults, Jessie. We have come to an agreement on the topic."

"Guess not everybody wins, huh?" Jessie looked over her shoulder, then back at you. "Like I said, the only thing worse than a happy Doran is a depressed Doran. If you're going to fuck around, then take responsibility. After all, you're very responsible, aren't you, _____?" She tossed her hair and walked back towards the camper tents.

Jessie's muddled affection for her brother was apparent. Maybe she was right. You were selfish. You were afraid. You didn't want to hurt him, and you didn't want to be hurt yourself. In a way, weren't you being more responsible by not using those three words so freely? And yet, the way that Doran stared out at the water made you think there was pain in never saying them at all.

The two of you performed your roles well for the next couple of days. Jessie seemed to be the only camper aware of the slight change in Doran's demeanor. Atticus noticed the change in Doran as well but figured that things were not finished between you two yet. That didn't stop him from digging one night as you sat together watching a horror marathon on a rabbit-ear TV in your cabin. "He said he loved you, didn't he?" he asked as you were gathering your clothes for the laundry.

"What?" You dropped your hiking socks.

"I knew it! Shit," he cursed as he looked away. "I told him to hold off, but he wouldn't listen."

"You knew?"

"Of course, I knew! It's Doran. How could he not love you?"

Your heart fumbled. "Does he," you feigned disinterest, "love a lot of people?"

"Practically everyone that walks the Earth."

You shriveled inside.

"No!" Atticus waved a hand in front of his face, "Not like that. He just cares. He wants people to see the bright side of life. But now he's just a void. I've never seen him act this way, really. It must be a different type of love."

You weren't sure how to feel about that. "He told me I didn't have to say it back."

"Do you… want to?"

"I don't know," you shook your head, "I'm not sure what will happen if I say it."

"I see. So, it's not about the relationship?"

"No, until a few days ago it was great."

"Ah. Listen, I know how it feels to be very passionate about somebody yet lose that feeling when the moment should be right. If it doesn't feel right, better to rip that bandage off now."

"It's not like that!" Your face flushed in defense.

Atticus blinked into a lazy smile. He stood up from the bed and dusted himself off. "Well, I learned not to play around with love. So, I'll leave the decisions up to you two. I'm off to finish this marathon in my cabin." He patted you on the shoulder on the way out. "Try not to think about it too hard. Love and logic aren't the best of friends. I mean, I can always be a rebound if you-"

"'Night, Atticus," you remarked.

"Loud and clear," he gave a sideways smile from the screen door. "Night, _____."

You gathered your items and headed for the washroom. In the twilight, the crickets began their summer song. The cicadas made the forest seem as if it were alive and humming. You admired the music of the night as you approached the laundry with one worn out washer and a dilapidated dryer. Nobody liked to do their laundry in the middle of the week, so it was your solitude. Any moment away from the kids was appreciated, even if it was spent doing chores.

Now it was just you, your laundry, and a book. You closed the door behind you and looked up towards the machines. *And Doran.* Apparently Doran.

"Oh," his face grew pale, and he tried to do several different things with his hands. "Hi! Hi, _____."

"Hi Dor." *Dor? Really? C'mon brain, do you have to make it more awkward?!*

He looked at you as if he'd seen a ghost.

"I'm sorry," you put a hand to your mouth. "I meant Doran. Gosh, I'm an idiot, you must not like being called that."

"That's... all right, really," He leaned against the washer where his clothes were completing their cycle. He was tall enough that his hips met the top with ease. "It's just that nobody has called me that in a long time." A faint smile returned to his face.

"You... used to be called Dor?'"

"Yeah," he gave a weak laugh as he rubbed his arm shyly. "I was a whole different person."

"Why don't you tell me more about it?"

He looked down. "It'd be a long story."

You pulled a busted plastic chair from the corner. "I've got time."

"Hah! You were a real troublemaker, weren't you? Just like Jessie."

You both shared a smile.

Doran sighed, "I was just acting out. Camp was the only place that felt like home, so I came back here every summer. I'm still here. I guess I never really grew up."

You put a hand on his shoulder in consolation. Somewhere along the way, you'd come to lean against the dryer with him. "You've become a fine man, Dor."

"How can you be so sure?" His eyes searched you.

"Because... You're the best person to be around. These past few days, I've realized that. I miss what we had before I went and screwed it all up by being awkward. I thought I was protecting myself, but I know you could never hurt me."

Doran shook his head as his brows furrowed. "Don't you see? I'm the one who messed up! I couldn't keep my feelings inside. I just had to go and say it. Still, I'm glad that you know. And I thought that I could deal with a one-sided love. But I want all of you. It hurts so much."

"Doran, I love you."

You could see his throat move as he swallowed, "I'm... sorry?"

"I love you," you pinned him against the dryer as you whispered in his ear.

His knees went weak as he shrank in front of you. "_____! What are you saying? Y-you don't love me, you've never loved anybody."

"I love *you*. And I can see that in the way I don't want you to hurt anymore. I want you more than I want to hide from this feeling."

"Are you lying?" His eyes were soft, as if he'd crumble.

"No, Doran," you shook your head.

In an instant he was upon you, lips crushing against yours with a fierceness you had yet to discover. Without even seeing how he'd done it, his adept hands removed your shirt and placed you on top of the dryer. You paused kissing to breathe for a moment, removing his shirt and wrapping your legs around his midsection to bring him flush against you. He kissed your neck delicately as he removed your bra.

"Say it again." His voice was almost gleeful as his hand hovered over your breast.

"I love you," your breath hitched as he traced his fingers lightly over your nipples. His repetitive movements were growing in intensity.

He moved himself between your legs, pulling your panties down along with your shorts. "Now add a 'Dor.' You said it so cutely before."

Your face flushed as you choked on the word, "I love you, Dor!"

His lips were upon you as your body writhed against his face, seeking the spot that made your stomach coil in pleasure. After a while he pulled back and wiped his lips with his hand. The innocent look returned to his face, "_____, are you mine? Can I have all of you?"

"All of me, Doran. Take me."

He pressed up against you gently, kissing you with a languid and growing pressure. You felt for him between kisses, rewarded by the hard warmth in your hand. He moaned into your mouth as you stroked him slowly. You both leaned back then and exchanged a glance before he aligned himself with your entrance, both hands resting on the other side of your thighs on the dryer. "I love you, _____." His voice was almost repentant as he pressed himself inside you. You groaned at the feeling only he could provide.

"Oh, Doran, yes!" You tossed your head back as he began to pump into you. Instinctively, he pressed a thumb against your clit as he moved back and forth. The friction he generated felt so good.

"_____," he whined as you placed kisses along his throat. Your hands sought his backside, bringing him deeper into you.

You inclined back to admire the rapturous look on his face before he leaned in and took your breast in his mouth. That did it for you, and you saw flashes of color as you rode him through waves of your orgasm.

"Ah! _____!" He whimpered as he pulled out, biting his lip as he came into your linens that would be thrown into the laundry. The sight set you ablaze all over again. He stood breathing from exertion as you sat atop the dryer trying to slow your heart.

You slid off and wrapped your arms around him. "That was amazing." You kissed his neck. His sweat was sweet.

"It was... Is this real?" He breathed into your hair.

"It really is," your fingers entwined. "And I'm so lucky you're mine."

He picked you up and spun you around, bringing you down slowly. "I'm going to spend every day making sure you're the happiest you can be. You won't regret loving me, _____, I promise."

"I know. That's why I love you, Doran." You smiled because that was all you truly could say. The washing machine buzzed its assent, and you couldn't help but laugh.

"Okay,   , what the hell did you do?" Jessie slammed her hands on the table at breakfast. "I know I told you that a depressed Doran was worse- but that was before I'd seen the likes of today." She leaned over towards you, "Have you seen this, have you?" She pointed to her head. "I have a fucking crown of clovers and it's nine in the morning!"

You snorted in laughter and sipped your coffee. "I was just being responsible."

"Responsible, my ass." Jessie plopped back into her seat.

"I like my crown!" Aisha patted the flowers. "Now I'm the queen of the forest!"

Josh sneezed, "I think I'm allergic..."

www.ingramcontent.com/pod-product-compliance
Lightning Source LLC
Chambersburg PA
CBHW060501130626
46555CB00017B/2748